Round about nine

poems for today

selected by Geoffrey Palmer & Noel Lloyd

with illustrations by Denis Wrigley

FREDERICK WARNE

Published by
FREDERICK WARNE & CO LTD: *London*
FREDERICK WARNE & CO INC: *New York*

For JAMES KIRKUP

LIBRARY OF CONGRESS CATALOG CARD NO 76–2921

ISBN 0 7232 1894 3

Printed in Great Britain by
Butler & Tanner Ltd
Frome and London
857.376

ROUND ABOUT NINE

poems for today

Contents

Acknowledgements

The compilers and publisher wish to thank the following for their kind permission to reproduce poems:

Eight and a Half
James MacGibbon, Executor of Stevie Smith, for 'My Cats' from *The Collected Poems of Stevie Smith* published by Allen Lane; James Kirkup for 'There Was an Old Man' and 'The Broken Toys', and 'Baby's Drinking Song' from *White Shadows, Black Shadows* published by J. M. Dent; The Acorn Press for 'Owl' from *The Poetical Ark* by Sylvia Read; Frances Evans for 'The Flying Horse'; Methuen Children's Books Ltd for 'The Tortoiseshell Cat' from *A Peck O'Maut* by Patrick Chalmers; Mrs A. M. Walsh for 'Sweet Chestnuts' from *The Roundabout by the Sea* by John Walsh; Angus & Robertson (U.K.) Ltd for 'Full Moon Rhyme' from *Songs for All Seasons* by Judith Wright; Granada Publishing Ltd for 'Neighbours' from *Daybreak* by Leonard Clark; The Estate of Robert Frost, the editor and Jonathan Cape Ltd for 'A Patch of Old Snow' from *The Poetry of Robert Frost*; Macmillan London & Basingstoke for 'Cow' from *Brownjohn's Beasts* by Alan Brownjohn; Martin Secker & Warburg Ltd for 'Christmas Day' from *Collected Poems by Andrew Young*, edited by Leonard Clark.
   'To a Squirrel at Kyle-Na-No' from *The Collected Poems of W. B. Yeats* is reprinted by permission of M. B. Yeats, Miss Anne Yeats, Macmillan Co. of Canada and Macmillan London & Basingstoke. Also reprinted with permission of Macmillan Publishing Co. Inc. from *Collected Poems* by William Butler Yeats. Copyright 1919 by Macmillan Publishing Co. Inc., renewed 1947 by Bertha Georgie Yeats. 'The Boy in the Barn' is reprinted by permission of Faber and Faber Ltd from *Collected Poems of Herbert Read*. 'Besides That', 'Danny Murphy' and 'Check' from *Collected Poems* by James Stephens are reprinted by permission of Mrs Iris Wise, Macmillan London & Basingstoke, and the Macmillan Co. of Canada. 'Besides That' is reprinted with permission of Macmillan Publishing Co. Inc. from *Collected Poems* by James Stephens. Copyright 1926 by Macmillan Publishing Co. Inc., renewed 1954 by Cynthia Stephens. 'Danny Murphy' is reprinted with permission of Macmillan Publishing Co. Inc. from *Collected Poems* by James Stephens. Copyright 1912 by Macmillan Publishing Co. Inc., renewed 1940 by James Stephens. 'Check' is reprinted with permission of Macmillan Publishing Co. Inc. from *Collected Poems* by James Stephens. Copyright 1915 by Macmillan Publishing Co. Inc., renewed 1943 by James Stephens. 'The East in Gold' from *The Complete Poems of W. H. Davies*, published by Jonathan Cape Ltd, is reprinted by permission of Mrs H. M. Davies and the Wesleyan University Press.

Nine and a Half
Clifford Dyment for 'Mouse' from *Poems 1935–48* published by J. M. Dent; The Enitharmon Press for 'Hedgehog' from *The Hearing Heart* by Leonard Clark; The Acorn Press for 'Peacock' from *The Poetical Ark* by Sylvia Read; the Daily Express for 'Idyll' from *The Best of Beachcomber* by J. B. Morton; F. T. Prince for 'Keeper's Wood' from *The Doors of Stone* published by Granada Publishing Ltd; James Kirkup for 'In a Strange House', 'Other People's Clothes' and 'Sleepwalker's Song'; Harry Graham for 'Quiet Fun' and Carelessness' from *More Ruthless Rhymes* published by Edward Arnold Ltd; Mrs A. M. Walsh for 'The Anemone' and 'The Boat' from *The Roundabout by the Sea* by John Walsh; James Reeves for 'The Toadstool Wood' from *The Blackbird in the Lilac* published by O.U.P.; The Estate of Robert Frost, the editor and Jonathan Cape Ltd for 'A Minor Bird' from *The Poetry of Robert Frost*; Miss Ann Wolfe for 'Green Candles' by Humbert Wolfe; Robert Graves for 'The P'eng That Was a K'un' from *Collected Poems 1965*.
   'The Waking' is reprinted by permission of Faber & Faber Ltd from *Collected Poems of Theodore Roethke*. 'The Waking', copyright 1948 by Theodore Roethke, from *The Collected Poems of Theodore Roethke*. Used by permission of Doubleday & Co. Inc. 'The Riddle' is reprinted by permission of Faber & Faber Ltd from *Collected Poems of Louis MacNeice*, and also from *The Collected Poems of Louis MacNeice*, edited by E. R. Dodds 1966. Copyright © The Estate of Louis MacNeice, 1966. Reprinted by permission of O.U.P., Inc. 'Blue Stars and Gold' from *Collected Poems* by James Stephens is reprinted by permission of Mrs Iris Wise, Macmillan London & Basingstoke, and the Macmillan Co. of Canada. Also reprinted with permission of Macmillan Co. Inc. from *Collected Poems* by James Stephens. Copyright 1915 by Macmillan Publishing Co. Inc., renewed 1943 by James Stephens.

Ten and a Half
Laurie Lee for an extract from 'Christmas Landscape' from *The Bloom of Candles* published by John Lehmann Ltd; Stephen Vincent Benet and Brandt & Brandt for 'Portrait of a Boy' from *Selected Works of Stephen Vincent Benét*; John Parke Custis Press for 'Leli' from *Sunshine Bar* by Noel Lloyd; Charles Causley for 'By St Thomas Water' from *Underneath the Water* published by Macmillan; Vernon Scannell for 'Hide and Seek' from *Walking Wounded* published by Eyre & Spottiswoode Ltd; James Kirkup for 'Who's That?'; The Literary Trustees of Walter de la Mare, and The Society of Authors as their representative, for 'The Ride-by-Nights' and 'Me' by Walter de la Mare; Norman MacCaid for 'Frogs' from *Surroundings* published by The Hogarth Press Ltd; The Enitharmon Press for 'Playthings' from *Masks and Ikons* by Kathleen Abbott; O.U.P. for 'Zodiac' from *The Children's Bells* by Eleanor Farjeon; the Executors of the Estate of C. Day Lewis for 'The Christmas Tree' from *Collected Poems 1954* published by Jonathan Cape Ltd and The Hogarth Press; Dorothy Rose Gribble and Plantagenet Productions for 'Joie-de-Vivre'.
   'who knows if the moon's a balloon' and 'maggie and milly and molly and may' from *The Complete Poems* by E. E. Cummings are reprinted by permission of Granada Publishing Ltd. 'who knows if the moon's a balloon' is copyright, 1925, by E. E. Cummings. Reprinted from *Complete Poems 1913–62*, by permission of Harcourt Brace Jovanovitch, Inc. 'maggie and milly and molly and may' is copyright © 1958 by E. E. Cummings. Reprinted from *Complete Poems 1913–62*, by permission of Harcourt Brace Jovanovich, Inc. 'The Principal Part of a Python' is from *The Reason for the Pelican* by John Ciardi. Copyright © 1959 by John Ciardi. Reprinted by permission of J. B. Lippincott Co. 'The Song of Wandering Aengus' from *The Collected Poems of W. B. Yeats* is reprinted by Macmillan Publishing Co. Inc. from *Collected Poems* by William Butler Yeats. Copyright 1906 by Macmillan Publishing Co. Inc., renewed 1934 by William Butler Yeats. 'Something Told the Wild Geese' is reprinted with permission of Macmillan Publishing Co. Inc. from *Poems* by Rachel Field. Copyright 1934 by Macmillan Publishing Co. Inc., renewed 1962 by Arthur S. Pederson. 'New Moon' from *The Complete Poems of D. H. Lawrence* published by William Heinemann Ltd is reprinted by permission of Laurence Pollinger Ltd and the Estate of the late Mrs Frieda Lawrence. Also reprinted from *The Complete Poems of D. H. Lawrence* by Vivian de Sola Pinto and F. Warren Roberts. Copyright 1964, 1971 by Angelo Ravagli and C. M. Weekley, Executors of the Estate of Frieda Lawrence Ravagli. All rights reserved. Reprinted by permission of the Viking Press, Inc. 'The Firefly' is copyright © 1963 by Paul Goodman. Reprinted from *Collected Poems*, by Paul Goodman, edited with preface by Taylor Stoehr, by permission of Random House, Inc.

   Whilst every effort has been made to trace the owners of copyrights, in a few cases this has proved impossible. We take this opportunity of tendering our apologies to any owners whose rights have been unwittingly infringed.

Eight
and a
half

Contents

My Cats

(A witch speaks)

I like to toss him up and down
A heavy cat weighs half a crown
With a hey do diddle my cat Brown.

I like to pinch him on the sly
When nobody is passing by
With a hey do diddle my cat Fry.

I like to ruffle up his pride
And watch him skip and turn aside
With a hey do diddle my cat Hyde.

Hey Brown and Fry and Hyde my cats
That sit on tombstones for your mats.

STEVIE SMITH

3

There Was an Old Man

There was an old man
Had a face made of cake,
He stuck it with currants
And put it in to bake.

The oven was hot,
He baked it too much,
It came out covered
With a crunchy crust.

The eyes went pop,
The currants went bang,
And that was the end
Of that old man.

JAMES KIRKUP

Owl

On Midsummer night the witches shriek,
The frightened fairies swoon,
The nightjar mutters in his sleep
And ghosts around the chimney creep.
The loud winds cry, the fir trees crash,
And the owl stares at the moon.

SYLVIA READ

For Saturday

Now's the time for mirth and play,
Saturday's an holiday;
Praise to heav'n unceasing yield,
I've found a lark's nest in the field.

A lark's nest, then your play-mate begs
You'd spare herself and speckled eggs;
Soon she shall ascend and sing
Your praises to th'eternal King.

CHRISTOPHER SMART

Spring

Sound the Flute!
Now it's mute.
Birds delight
Day and Night;
Nightingale
In the dale
Lark in Sky,
Merrily,
Merrily, Merrily, to welcome in the Year.

Little Boy,
Full of joy;
Little Girl,
Sweet and small;
Cock does crow,
So do you;
Merry voice,
Infant noise,
Merrily, Merrily, to welcome in the Year.

Little Lamb,
Here I am;
Come and lick
My white neck;
Let me pull
Your soft Wool;
Let me kiss
Your soft face:
Merrily, Merrily, we welcome in the Year.

WILLIAM BLAKE

6

The Flying Horse

The flying horse
In majesty
Scorned the earth
With hooves of fire.
His mane shone gold,
His coat glowed bright;
The Jade Princess
Rejoiced to fly.

Swift as the wind
He bore her away,
Into the sky
And eternity.

FRANCES EVANS

FROM The Skies Can't Keep Their Secret

The Skies can't keep their secret!
They tell it to the Hills—
The Hills just tell the Orchards—
And they—the Daffodils!

A Bird—by chance—that goes that way—
Soft overhears the whole—
If I should bribe the little Bird—
Who knows but *she* would tell?

EMILY DICKINSON

7

The Tortoiseshell Cat

The tortoiseshell cat
She sits on the mat,
As gay as a sunflower she;
In orange and black you see her blink,
And her waistcoat's white, and her nose is pink,
And her eyes are green of the sea.
But all is vanity, all the way;
Twilight's coming and close of day,
And every cat in the twilight's grey,
Every possible cat.

The tortoiseshell cat
She is smooth and fat,
And we call her Josephine,
Because she weareth upon her back
This coat of colours, this raven black,
This red of the tangerine.
But all is vanity, all the way;
Twilight follows the brightest day,
And every cat in the twilight's grey,
Every possible cat.

PATRICK CHALMERS

To a Squirrel at Kyle-Na-No

Come play with me;
Why should you run
Through the shaking tree
As though I'd a gun
To strike you dead?
When all I would do
Is to scratch your head
And let you go.

W. B. YEATS

Baby's Drinking Song

(For a baby learning for the first time to drink from a cup)

Sip a little
Sup a little
    From your little
Cup a little
    Sup a little
Sip a little
    Put it to your
Lip a little
    Tip a little
Tap a little
    Not into your
Lap or it'll
    Drip a little
Drop a little
    On the table
Top a little.

JAMES KIRKUP

Besides That

If I could get to heaven
By eating all I could,
I'd become a pig,
And I'd gobble up my food!

Or, if I could get to heaven
By climbing up a tree,
I'd become a monkey,
And I'd climb up rapidly!

Or, if I could get to heaven
By any other way
Than the way that's told of,
I'd 'a been there yesterday!

But the way that we are told of
Bars the monkey and the pig!
And is very, very difficult,
Besides that!

JAMES STEPHENS

The Duel

The gingham dog and the calico cat
Side by side on the table sat;
'Twas half past twelve, and (what do you think!)
Nor one nor t'other had slept a wink!
  The old Dutch clock and the Chinese plate
  Appeared to know as sure as fate
There was going to be a terrible spat.
  (*I wasn't there; I simply state
  What was told to me by the Chinese plate!*)

The gingham dog went 'Bow-wow-wow!'
And the calico cat replied 'Mee-ow!'
The air was littered, an hour or so,
With bits of gingham and calico,
  While the old Dutch clock in the chimney-place
  Up with its hands before its face,
For it always dreaded a family row!
  (*Now mind: I'm only telling you
  What the old Dutch clock declares is true!*)

The Chinese plate looked very blue,
And wailed: 'Oh, dear! what shall we do?'
But the gingham dog and the calico cat
Wallowed this way and tumbled that,
    Employing every tooth and claw
    In the awfullest way you ever saw—
And, oh! how the gingham and calico flew!
    (*Don't fancy I exaggerate!*
    I got my news from the Chinese plate!)

Next morning, where the two had sat,
They found no trace of dog or cat;
And some folks think unto this day
That burglars stole that pair away!
    But the truth about that cat and pup
    Is this: they ate each other up!
Now what do you really think of that!
    (*The old Dutch clock it told me so,*
    And that is how I came to know.)

EUGENE FIELD

Gipsies

The gipsies seek wide sheltering woods again,
With droves of horses flock to mark their lane,
And trample on dead leaves, and hear the sound,
And look and see the black clouds gather round,
And set their camps, and free from muck and mire,
And gather stolen sticks to make the fire.
The roasted hedgehog, bitter though as gall,
Is eaten up and relished by them all.
They know the woods and every fox's den
And get their living far away from men;
The shooters ask them where to find the game,
The rabbits know them and are almost tame.
The aged women, tawny with the smoke,
Go with the winds and crack the rotted oak.

JOHN CLARE

Sweet Chestnuts

How still the woods were! Not a redbreast whistled
To mark the end of a mild autumn day.
Under the trees the chestnut-cases lay,
Looking like small green hedgehogs softly bristled.

Plumply they lay, each with its fruit packed tight;
For when we rolled them gently with our feet,
The outer shells burst wide apart and split,
Showing the chestnuts brown and creamy-white.

Quickly we kindled a bright fire of wood,
And placed them in the ashes. There we sat,
Listening how all our chestnuts popped and spat.
And then, the smell how rich, the taste how good!

JOHN WALSH

Full Moon Rhyme

There's a hare in the moon tonight,
crouching alone in the bright
buttercup field of the moon;
and all the dogs in the world
howl at the hare in the moon.

'I chased that hare to the sky,'
the hungry dogs all cry.
'The hare jumped into the moon
and left me here in the cold.
I chased that hare to the moon.'

'Come down again, mad hare,
we can see you there,'
the dogs all howl to the moon.
'Come down again to the world,
you mad black hare in the moon,

or we will grow wings and fly
up to the star-grassed sky
to hunt you out of the moon,'
the hungry dogs of the world
howl at the hare in the moon.

JUDITH WRIGHT

16

The Boy in the Barn

A little boy wandering alone in the night
Went in a barn all wrecked and decayed;
And the bats and the moths and the fluttering things
Flew in his face and made him afraid.

So he fell on the floor and buried his head,
And his lantern fell down at his feet;
And he heard as he lay on the sweet-smelling hay
His little heart beat, beat, beat . . .

O little boy lift your light aloft
And the bats will scamper away;
And the big brown moths will kiss the flame
And flutter down dead on the sweet-smelling hay.

HERBERT READ

Queen Nefertiti

Spin a coin, spin a coin,
All fall down;
Queen Nefertiti
Stalks through the town.

Over the pavements
Her feet go clack,
Her legs are as tall
As a chimney stack.

Her fingers flicker
Like snakes in the air,
The walls split open
At her green-eyed stare.

Her voice is thin
As the ghosts of bees;
She will crumble your bones,
She will make your blood freeze.

Spin a coin, spin a coin,
All fall down;
Queen Nefertiti
Stalks through the town.

UNKNOWN

Gulliver in Lilliput

From his nose
Clouds he blows.
When he speaks,
Thunder breaks.
When he eats,
Famine threats.
When he treads,
Mountains' heads
Groan and shake;
Armies quake.
See him stride
Valleys wide,
Over woods,
Over floods.
Troops take heed,
Man and steed:
Left and right,
Speed your flight!
In amaze
Lost I gaze
Toward the skies:
See! and believe your eyes!

ALEXANDER POPE

Danny Murphy

He was as old as old could be,
His little eye could scarcely see,
His mouth was sunken in between
His nose and chin, and he was lean
And twisted up and withered quite,
So that he couldn't walk aright.

His pipe was always going out,
And then he'd have to search about
In all his pockets, and he'd mow
—O, deary me! and, musha now!—
And then he'd light his pipe, and then
He'd let it go clean out again.

He couldn't dance or jump or run,
Or ever have a bit of fun
Like me and Susan, when we shout
And jump and throw ourselves about:
—But when he laughed, then you could see
He was as young as young could be!

JAMES STEPHENS

20

Neighbours

The people who live on the right of us
Are very quiet and make no fuss,
But the family on the left clatter about
Day and night, and sometimes shout.

Yet the people on the left of us
Are really rather marvellous,
Instead of being put out by everything
They burst out laughing and sing.

But the family who live on the right of us
Often make me curious,
The way the father whispers to the mother,
The sister to her silent brother.

I suppose that neighbours are meant
To be different.

LEONARD CLARK

Check

The night was creeping on the ground;
She crept and did not make a sound
Until she reached the tree, and then
She covered it, and stole again
Along the grass beside the wall.

I heard the rustle of her shawl
As she threw blackness everywhere
Upon the sky and ground and air,
And in the room where I was hid:
But no matter what she did
To everything that was without,
She could not put my candle out.

So I stared at the night, and she
Stared back solemnly at me.

JAMES STEPHENS

Birthday

It's my birthday today,
And I'm nine.
I'm having a party tonight,
And we'll play on the lawn
If it's fine.
There'll be John, Dick and Jim,
And Alan and Tim,
And Dennis and Brian and Hugh;
But the star of the show,
You'll be sorry to know,
Will be Sue.
(She's my sister, aged two,
And she'll yell till she's blue
In the face, and be sick).

UNKNOWN

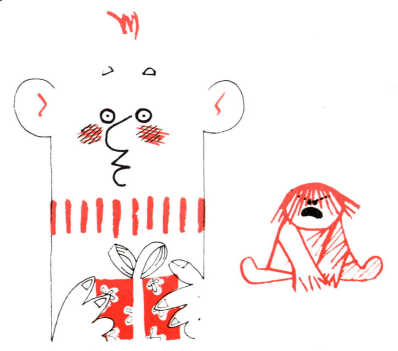

23

The Broken Toys

In the broken box
The broken toys—
    Dusty,
Battered and rusty,
Tattered and torn,
    Forlorn, forlorn.

The snapped strings
And the busted springs,
The rag-doll raggy and rent,
The pink tin teaset buckled and bent,
    The crashed plane,
    The car, the train—
Smashed in a terrible accident.

And all the dolls' eyes
Rolling loose like heavy marbles
Up the doll's house stairs and down
The stairs of the overturned house . . .
The dead wheels of a clockwork mouse . . .

In the broken box
The broken toys—
    Dusty,
Battered and rusty,
Tattered and torn,
    Forlorn, forlorn.

JAMES KIRKUP

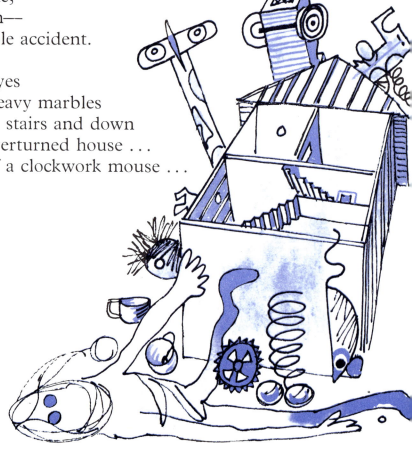

A Patch of Old Snow

There's a patch of old snow in a corner
    That I should have guessed
Was a blow-away paper the rain
    Had brought to rest.

It is speckled with grime as if
    Small print overspread it,
The news of a day I've forgotten—
    If I ever read it.

ROBERT FROST

The East in Gold

Somehow this world is wonderful at times,
As it has been from early morn in May;
Since first I heard the cock-a-doodle-do—
Timekeeper on green farms—at break of day.

Soon after that I heard ten thousand birds,
Which made me think an angel brought a bin
Of golden grain, and none was scattered yet—
To rouse those birds to make that merry din.

I could not sleep again, for such wild cries,
And went out early into their green world;
And then I saw what set their little tongues
To scream for joy—they saw the East in gold.

W. H. DAVIES

Once I Was a Monarch's Daughter

Once I was a monarch's daughter,
And sat on a lady's knee:
But now I am a nightly rover
Banished to the ivy tree.

Crying *hoo, hoo, hoo, hoo, hoo,*
Hoo, hoo, hoo, my feet are cold.

Pity me, for here you see me
Persecuted, poor, and old.

UNKNOWN

Cow

You wouldn't think so solid an animal could be
  so learned.
You wouldn't think my big empty eyes could
  understand so much.
You wouldn't think my slow ways could hide
  such rapid thinking.
You wouldn't think my voice could express
  wonderful thoughts if it wanted to.
You wouldn't think I was ever planning things
  while I was chewing,
would you?

Look out for yourselves, I am simply waiting my
  time.

ALAN BROWNJOHN

A Fishing Song

There was a boy whose name was Phinn,
And he was fond of fishing;
His father could not keep him in,
Nor all his mother's wishing.

His life's ambition was to land
A fish of several pound weight;
The chief thing he could understand,
Was hooks, or worms for ground-bait.

The worms crept out, the worms crept in,
From every crack and pocket;
He had a worm-box made of tin,
With proper worms to stock it.

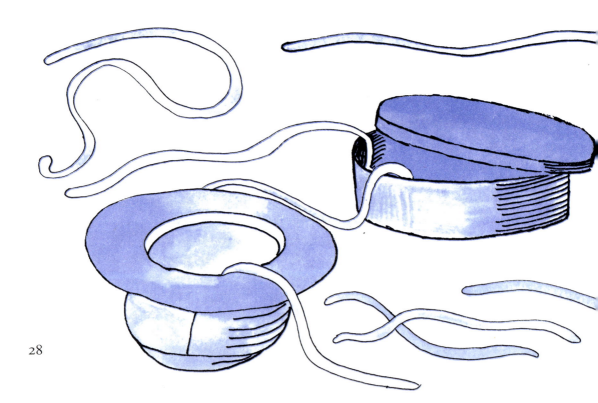

28

He gave his mind to breeding worms
As much as he was able;
His sister spoke in angry terms
To see them on the table.

You found one walking up the stairs,
You found one in a bonnet,
Or, in the bedroom, unawares,
You set your foot upon it.

Worms, worms, worms for bait!
Roach, and dace, and gudgeon!
With rod and line to Twickenham Ait
Tomorrow he is trudging!

O worms and fishes day and night!
Such was his sole ambition;
I'm glad to think you are not quite
So very fond of fishing!

WILLIAM BRIGHTY RANDS

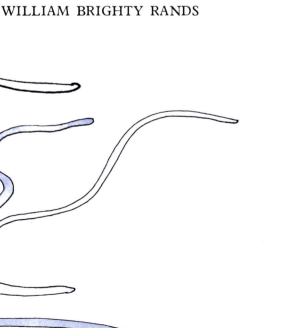

The Carol of the Poor Children

We are the poor children, come out to see the sights
On this day of all days, on this night of nights:
The stars in merry parties are dancing in the sky,
A fine star, a new star, is shining on high!

We are the poor children, our lips are frosty blue,
We cannot sing our carol as well as rich folk do:
Our bellies are so empty we have no singing voice,
But this night of all nights good children must rejoice.

We do rejoice, we do rejoice, as hard as we can try,
A fine star, a new star is shining in the sky!
And while we sing our carol, we think of the delight
The happy kings and shepherds make in Bethlehem tonight.

Are we naked, mother, and are we starving-poor—
Oh, see what gifts the kings have brought outside the stable door.
Are we cold, mother, the ass will give his hay
To make the manger warm and keep the cruel winds away.

We are the poor children, but not so poor who sing
Our carol with our voiceless hearts to greet the new-born king:
On this night of all nights, when in the frosty sky
A new star, a kind star is shining on high!

RICHARD MIDDLETON

Christmas Day

Last night in the open shippen
    The Infant Jesus lay,
While cows stood at the hay-crib
    Twitching the sweet hay.

As I trudged through the snow-fields
    That lay in their own light,
A thorn-bush with its shadow
    Stood doubled on the night.

And I stayed on my journey
    To listen to the cheep
Of a small bird in the thorn-bush
    I woke from its puffed sleep.

The bright stars were my angels
    And with the heavenly host
I sang praise to the Father,
    The Son and Holy Ghost.

ANDREW YOUNG

Nine
and a
half

Contents

FROM **Winter**

Bite, frost, bite!
You roll up away from the light
The blue wood-louse, and the plump dormouse,
And the bees are stilled, and the flies are killed,
And you bite hard into the heart of the house,
But not into mine.

LORD TENNYSON

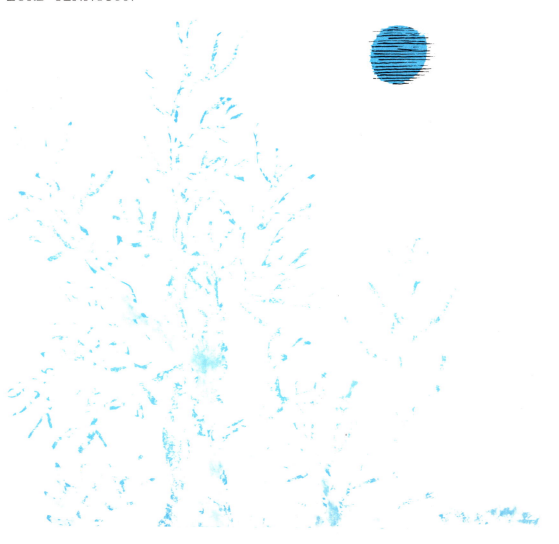

January

Cold the day and cold the drifted snow,
Dim the day until the cold dark night.
Crackle, sparkle, faggot; embers glow:
Some one may be plodding through the snow
Longing for a light,
For the light that you and I can show.
If no one else should come,
Here Robin Redbreast's welcome to a crumb,
And never troublesome:
Robin, why don't you come and fetch your crumb?

Here's butter for my hunch of bread,
    And sugar for your crumb;
Here's room upon the hearthrug,
    If you'll only come.

In your scarlet waistcoat,
    With your keen bright eye,
Where are you loitering?
    Wings were made to fly!

Make haste to breakfast,
    Come and fetch your crumb,
For I'm as glad to see you
    As you are glad to come.

CHRISTINA ROSSETTI

36

Travel

I should like to rise and go
Where the golden apples grow;
Where below another sky
Parrot islands anchored lie,
And, watched by cockatoos and goats,
Lonely Crusoes building boats;
Where in sunshine reaching out
Eastern cities, miles about,
Are with mosque and minaret
Among sandy gardens set,
And the rich goods from near and far
Hang for sale in the bazaar;
Where the Great Wall round China goes,
And on one side the desert blows,
And with bell and voice and drum,
Cities on the other hum;
Where are forests, hot as fire,
Wide as England, tall as a spire,
Full of apes and coconuts
And the negro hunters' huts;
Where the knotty crocodile
Lies and blinks in the Nile,
And the red flamingo flies
Hunting fish before his eyes;
Where in jungles, near and far,
Man-devouring tigers are,
Lying close and giving ear
Lest the hunt be drawing near,
Or a comer-by be seen
Swinging in a palanquin;
Where among the desert sands
Some deserted city stands,

All its children, sweep and prince,
Grown to manhood ages since,
Not a foot in street or house,
Not a stir of child or mouse,
And when kindly falls the night,
In all the town no spark of light.
There I'll come when I'm a man
With a camel caravan;
Light a flower in the gloom
Of some dusty dining-room;
See the pictures on the walls,
Heroes, fights, and festivals;
And in a corner find the toys
Of the old Egyptian boys.

ROBERT LOUIS STEVENSON

Mouse

I cursed the mouse that gnawed my cheese
And trespassed smoothly on my peace.

I growled and vowed I'd do him in—
The wretched scrap of speed and sin!

'You haunt my dreams and days,' I cried;
'For my bread's sake it's time you died!'

I laughed to find my cunning trap
Had killed the beastly little chap.

The little chap! Yes, that's the name
I used in death and stood in shame.

The story of that righteous deed
Is now a sword on which I bleed.

CLIFFORD DYMENT

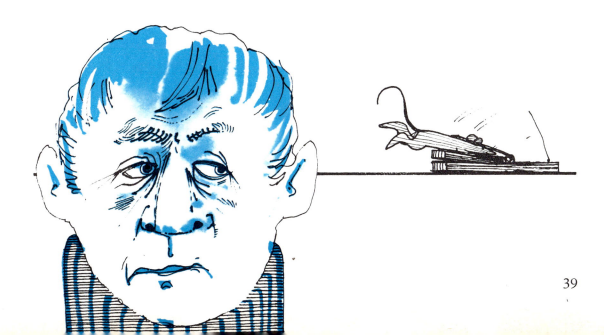

The Waking

I strolled across
An open field;
The sun was out;
Heat was happy.

This way! This way!
The wren's throat shimmered,
Either to other,
The blossoms sang.

The stones sang,
The little ones did,
And flowers jumped
Like small goats.

A ragged fringe
Of daisies waved;
I wasn't alone
In a grove of apples.

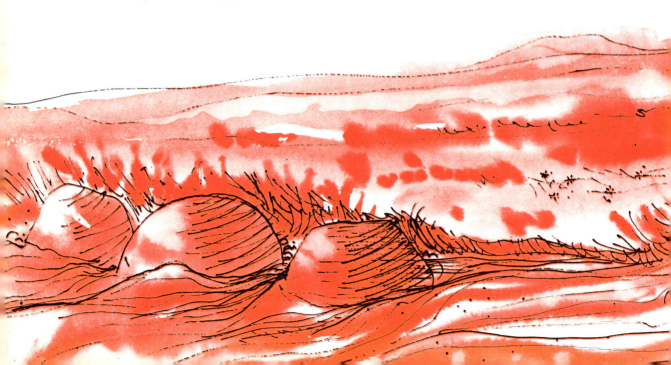

Far in the wood
A nestling sighed;
The dew loosened
Its morning smells.

I came where the river
Ran over stones:
My ears knew
An early joy.

And all the waters
Of all the streams
Sang in my veins
That summer day.

THEODORE ROETHKE

Hedgehog

Comes out by day in autumn,
exploring hedgehog, betrays himself
snoring loudly in leafy ditch;
plump with summer's fat, moves along,
battering slow way through dry twigs.
I hear him lumbering, hairy head appears,
then all his ten-inch prickly length,
makes for the bank, senses me there,
rolls into a ball, waits for the attack.
I leave him alone though, curled up on the hill's lip,
this earth-brown savage, enemy of frogs.
He'll chew beetles and mice to powder, hear
every small noise in undergrowth,
will take on snakes by the tail,
bayonet them with needle-spines.
Shy of the sun, dislikes company,
cannot see far, a fine swimmer,
drinks milk.

LEONARD CLARK

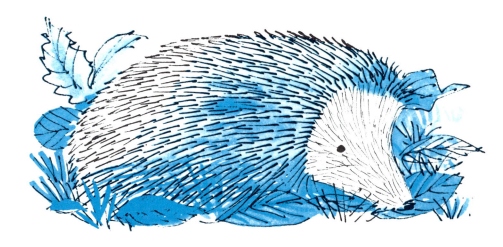

Peacock

The peacock, like a waterfall,
Lets flow his coloured tail,
Where eyes like stars are winking bright
Through the dark gardens of the night
In palaces for man's delight.
But when he walks and proudly shows
His tail outspread, the peacock goes
Like a bright galley rigged and tall,
A thousand jewels in his sail.

SYLVIA READ

Steam Shovel

The dinosaurs are not all dead.
I saw one raise its iron head
To watch me walking down the road
Beyond our house today.
Its jaws were dripping with a load
Of earth and grass that it had cropped.
It must have heard me where I stopped,
Snorted white steam my way,
And stretched its long neck out to see,
And chewed, and grinned quite amiably.

CHARLES MALAM

Idyll

I knew a child called Alma Brent,
    Completely destitute of brains,
Whose principal accomplishment
Was imitating railway trains.

When ladies called at 'Sunnyside',
Mama, to keep the party clean,
Would say, with pardonable pride,
    'Now, Alma, do the six-fifteen.'

The child would grunt and snort and puff,
With weird contortions of the face,
And when the guests had had enough,
She'd cease, with one last wild grimace.

One day her jovial Uncle Paul
    Cried, 'Come on, Alma! Do your worst!'
And, challenged thus before them all,
    She did the four-nineteen—and burst.

J. B. MORTON

44

Clock-a-Clay

(Ladybird)

In the cowslip pips I lie,
Hidden from the buzzing fly,
While green grass beneath me lies,
Pearled with dew like fishes' eyes,
Here I lie, a clock-a-clay,
Waiting for the time of day.

While the forest quakes surprise,
And the wild wind sobs and sighs,
My home ricks are like to fall,
On its pillar green and tall;
When the pattering rain drives by
Clock-a-clay keeps warm and dry.

Day by day and night by night,
All the week I hide from sight;
In the cowslip pips I lie,
In rain and dew still warm and dry;
Day and night, and night and day,
Red, black-spotted clock-a-clay.

My home shakes in wind and showers,
Pale green pillar topped with flowers,
Bending at the wild wind's breath,
Till I touch the grass beneath,
Here I live, lone clock-a-clay,
Watching for the time of day.

JOHN CLARE

Keeper's Wood

Within these dusky woods
The blackthorn hides.
The violets in the rides
On a grey day
Among pale primrose-buds
Crouch, hidden away.

A loud jay curses all.
A gust goes by
Under the cloud-cold sky,
And as you walk,
In the fields the lambs call,
And the rooks talk.

F. T. PRINCE

The Key of the Kingdom

This is the key of the kingdom.
In that kingdom there is a city;
In that city there is a town;
In that town there is a street;
In that street there is a lane;
In that lane there is a yard;
In that yard there is a house;
In that house there is a room;
In that room there is a bed;
On that bed there is a basket;
In that basket there are some flowers.

Flowers in the basket;
Basket on the bed;
Bed in the room;
Room in the house;
House in the yard;
Yard in the lane;
Lane in the street;
Street in the town;
Town in the city;
City in the kingdom.
This is the key of the kingdom.

UNKNOWN

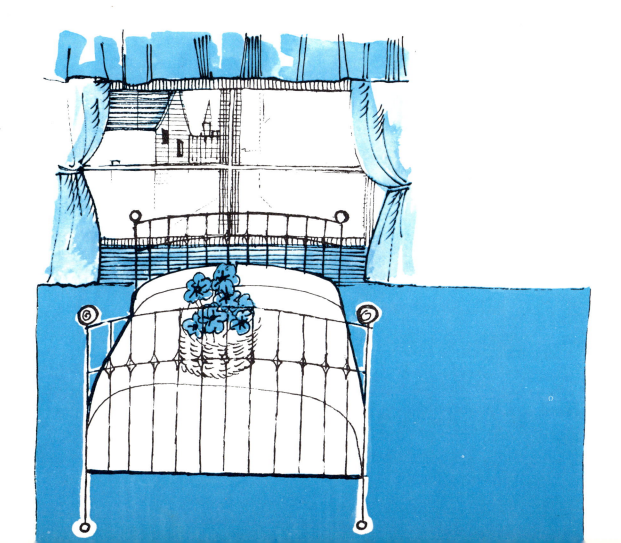

The Riddle

'What is it that goes round and round the house'
The riddle began. A wolf, we thought, or a ghost?
Our cold backs turned to the chink in the kitchen shutter,
The range made our small scared faces warm as toast.

But now the cook is dead and the cooking, no doubt, electric,
No room for draught and dream, for child or mouse,
Though we, in another place, still put ourselves the question:
What *is* it that goes round and round the house?

LOUIS MACNEICE

In a Strange House

Stranger, open the door is one,
And wipe your feet on the mat is two,
(For this is the only house he knows
Where no one but his own self goes).

Creep up the twisty stairs is three,
Turn on the light is four,
Take off your hat and coat is five,
And six, be glad you're still alive.

Draw the red curtains is number seven,
Sit by the fire is eight,
Cover the canary is nine, and ten
Is wind up the clock, it's getting late!

Eleven is when your prayers are said,
And twelve is tuck yourself in bed—
(For this is the only house he knows
Where no one but his own self goes).

JAMES KIRKUP

Tom Thumb's Epitaph

Here lies Tom Thumb, King Arthur's Knight,
Who died by a spider's cruel bite.
He was well known in Arthur's court,
Where he afforded gallant sport.
He rode at tilt and tournament,
And on a mouse a-hunting went.
Alive he filled the court with mirth;
His death to sorrow soon gave birth.
Wipe, wipe your eyes and shake your head
And cry, 'Alas! Tom Thumb is dead!'

UNKNOWN

Quiet Fun

My son Augustus, in the street, one day,
   Was feeling quite exceptionally merry.
A stranger asked him: 'Can you show me, pray,
   The quickest way to Brompton Cemetery?'
'The quickest way? You bet I can!' said Gus,
And pushed the fellow underneath a bus.

Whatever people say about my son,
He does enjoy his little bit of fun.

HARRY GRAHAM

The Faery Song

How beautiful they are,
The lordly ones
Who dwell in the hills,
In the hollow hills.

They have faces like flowers
And their breath is a wind
That blows over summer meadows
Filled with dewy clover.

Their limbs are more white
Than shafts of moonshine,
They are more fleet than the March wind.

They laugh and are glad,
And are terrible;
When their lances shake and glitter
Every green reed quivers.

How beautiful they are,
The lordly ones
Who dwell in the hills.
In the hollow hills.

FIONA MACLEOD

Other People's Clothes

Overcoat hanging on the door,
Why do you fall upon the floor?

Cloth cap hanging on a hook,
Why do you give me such a look?

Gloves that hold hands on the shelf,
Why do you make me talk to myself?

Clogs, great clogs upon the rack,
Why do you stamp when I turn my back?

    I'll put on the coat,
    I'll put on the hat,
    I'll put on the gloves
    (Though they're far too fat).

I'll even put on the great black clogs
And clump down the streets with the cats and dogs

Shouting beneath the carnival flags
'Rags! Rags! Any old rags?'

JAMES KIRKUP

52

The Twins

In form and feature, face and limb,
I grew so like my brother,
That folks got taking me for him,
And each for one another.
It puzzled all our kith and kin,
It reach'd an awful pitch;
For one of us was born a twin,
Yet not a soul knew which.

One day (to make the matter worse),
Before our names were fix'd,
As we were being wash'd by nurse
We got completely mix'd;
And thus, you see, by Fate's decree
(Or rather nurse's whim),
My brother John got christen'd *me*,
And I got christen'd *him*.

This fatal likeness even dogg'd
My footsteps when at school,
And I was always getting flogg'd
For John turn'd out a fool.
I put this question hopelessly
To every one I knew—
What *would* you do, if you were me,
To prove that you were *you*?

Our close resemblance turn'd the tide
Of my domestic life;
For somehow my intended bride
Became my brother's wife.
In short, year after year the same
Absurd mistakes went on;
And when I died—the neighbours came
And buried brother John!

HENRY SAMBROOKE LEIGH

The Anemone

Under this ledge of rock a brown
And soft anemone clings,
Spreading his fingers to the sea
Deliciously.
I kneel down on the sand,
And squeezing gently with my thumb
I loose his hold and take him in my hand.
But now how swift his fingers are withdrawn!—
His tendrils shrunk and gone!
I dabble him and water him in vain—
He will not flower again;
And though I press him firmly to his rock,
He will not stick again or cling,
But sinks disconsolately down,
And is lost, poor thing!

JOHN WALSH

The Toadstool Wood

The toadstool wood is dark and mouldy,
　And has a ferny smell.
About the trees hangs something quiet
　And queer—like a spell.

Beneath the arching sprays of bramble
　Small creatures make their holes;
Over the moss's close green velvet
　The stilted spider strolls.

The stalks of toadstools pale and slender
　That grow from that old log,
Bars they might be to imprison
　A prince turned to a frog.

There lives no mumbling witch nor wizard
　In this uncanny place,
Yet you might think you saw at twilight
　A little, crafty face.

JAMES REEVES

55

The Boat

Today has brought us to our heart's wish;
On narrow stream between high banks afloat,
We urge along our sun-soaked, paint-worn,
Lolloping boat.

Above, the bank-tops, purple- and cream-flowered!
Beyond, unseen, the harvest-fields expand;
But here we navigate a new
And watery land.

Here are no fringing flowers, no corn, but only
The bare tree-roots and all the muddied, grey,
Down-dropping leaves from which the floods
Have sunk away.

Let's rest our paddles; we have time to spend—
Time, if we wish, to watch some bank-side hole,
Glimpsing, perhaps, the peer and twitch
Of a whiskered vole.

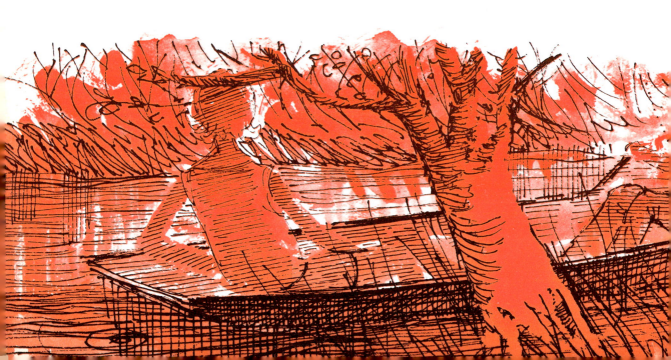

Or we may search for lily-cups, up-twist
The slimy root-stems from their oozy bed;
Or chase the blue kingfisher, flitting
Always ahead.

Or find again that narrowest stream of all—
That rushy pad where once a nesting swan
Sat out the spring. We'll pause, then creep
Windingly on;

And not turn back till evening, when a wind
Troubles our shadowy water, and a sigh
Hissles the sheaves of sunset corn
Stacked on the sky.

JOHN WALSH

The Useful Plough

A country life is sweet,
In moderate cold and heat,
To walk in the air, how pleasant and fair,
In ev'ry field of wheat.
The fairest of flowers adorning the bowers
And ev'ry meadow's brow;
So that, I say, no courtier may
Compare with them who clothe in grey,
And follow the useful plough.

They rise with the morning lark,
And labour till almost dark,
Then folding their sheep, they hasten to sleep,
While ev'ry pleasant park
Next morning is ringing with birds that are singing,
On each green tender bough.
With what content and merriment
Their days are spent, whose minds are bent
To follow the useful plough.

UNKNOWN

58

A Minor Bird

I have wished a bird would fly away,
And not sing by my house all day;

Have clapped my hands at him from the door
When it seemed as if I could bear no more.

The fault must partly have been in me.
The bird was not to blame for his key.

And of course there must be something wrong
In wanting to silence any song.

ROBERT FROST

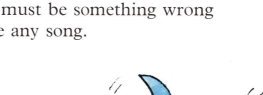

Carelessness

A window-cleaner in our street
Who fell (five storeys) at my feet
Impaled himself on my umbrella.
I said, 'Come, come, you careless fella!
If my umbrella had been shut
You might have landed on my nut!'

HARRY GRAHAM

Green Candles

'There's someone at the door,' said gold candlestick:
'Let her in quick, let her in quick!'
'There is a small hand groping at the handle:
Why don't you turn it?' asked green candle.

'Don't go, don't go,' said the Hepplewhite chair,
'Lest you find a strange lady there.'
'Yes, stay where you are,' whispered the white wall:
'There is nobody there at all.'

'I know her little foot,' grey carpet said:
'Who but I should know her light tread?'
'She shall come in,' answered the open door,
'And not,' said the room, 'go out any more.'

HUMBERT WOLFE

The P'eng that was a K'un

(Adapted from the Chinese of Lao Tse)

In Northern seas there roams a fish called a K'un,
Of how many thousand leagues in length I know not,
Which changes to a bird called P'eng—its wing-span
Of how many thousand leagues in width I know not.
Every half-year this P'eng, that was a K'un,
Fans out its glorious feathers to the whirlwind
And soars to the most Southerly pool of Heaven.

The Finch and Sparrow, thus informed, debated:
'We by our utmost efforts may fly only
To yonder elm. How can a P'eng outdo us?
Though, indeed, neither started as a fish.'

ROBERT GRAVES

The Barn Owl

While moonlight, silvering all the walls,
Through every mouldering crevice falls,
Tipping with white his powdery plume,
As shades or shifts the changing gloom;
The Owl that, watching in the barn,
Sees the mouse creeping in the corn,
Sits still and shuts his round blue eyes
As if he slept—until he spies
The little beast within his stretch—
Then starts—and seizes on the wretch!

SAMUEL BUTLER

Blue Stars and Gold

While walking through the trams and cars
I chanced to look up at the sky,
And saw that it was full of stars!

So starry-sown! A man could not,
With any care, have stuck a pin
Through any single vacant spot.

And some were shining furiously;
And some were big and some were small;
But all were beautiful to see.

Blue stars and gold! A sky of grey!
The air between a velvet pall!
I could not take my eyes away!

And there I sang this little psalm
Most awkwardly! Because I was
Standing between a car and tram!

JAMES STEPHENS

Sleepwalker's Song

Feet on the floor
Hand at the door
Eye at the window
Sleeping sleeping

Still are the stairs
High is the room
Cool is the mirror
Looking looking

Wild is the moor
Dark is the air
Late is the morning
Breaking breaking

Bitter my dream
And fearful the scream
Of the sea-bird
Weeping weeping

Heavy my tread
And stony the bed
Where I shall be laid
Waking waking

JAMES KIRKUP

Ten and a half

Contents

FROM **Christmas Landscape**

Tonight the wind gnaws
with teeth of glass,
the jackdaw shivers
in caged branches of iron,
the stars have talons.

There is hunger in the mouth
of vole and badger,
silver agonies of breath
in the nostril of the fox,
ice on the rabbit's paw.

Tonight has no moon,
no food for the pilgrim;
the fruit tree is bare,
the rose bush a thorn
and the ground bitter with stones.

But the mole sleeps, and the hedgehog
lies curled in a womb of leaves,
the bean and the wheat-seed
hug their germs in the earth
and the stream moves under the ice.

Tonight there is no moon,
but a new star opens
like a silver trumpet over the head.
Tonight in a nest of ruins
the blessed babe is laid.

LAURIE LEE

FROM **The Princess**

The splendour falls on castle walls
  And snowy summits old in story;
The long light shakes across the lakes,
  And the wild cataract leaps in glory.
Blow, bugle, blow, set the wild echoes flying,
Blow, bugle; answer, echoes, dying, dying, dying.

O hark, O hear! how thin and clear,
  And thinner, clearer, farther going!
O, sweet and far from cliff and scar
  The horns of Elfland faintly blowing!
Blow, let us hear the purple glens replying,
Blow, bugle; answer, echoes, dying, dying, dying.

O love, they die in yon rich sky,
  They faint on hill or field or river;
Our echoes roll from soul to soul,
  And grow for ever and for ever.
Blow, bugle, blow, set the wild echoes flying,
And answer, echoes, answer, dying, dying, dying.

LORD TENNYSON

68

Portrait of a Boy

After the whipping he crawled into bed,
Accepting harsh fact with no great weeping.
How funny uncle's hat had looked striped red!
He chuckled silently. The moon came, sweeping
A black, frayed rag of tattered cloud before
In scorning; very pure and pale she seemed,
Flooding his bed with radiance. On the floor
Fat moths danced. He sobbed, closed his eyes and dreamed.

Warm sand flowed round him. Blurts of crimson light
Splashed the white grains like blood. Past the cave's mouth
Shone with a large, fierce, splendour, wildly bright,
The crooked constellations of the South;
Here the Cross swung; and there, affronting Mars,
The Centaur stormed aside a froth of stars.
Within, great casks, like wattled aldermen,
Sighed of enormous feasts, and cloth of gold
Glowed on the walls like hot desire. Again,
Beside webbed purples from some galleon's hold,
A black chest bore the skull and bones in white
Above a scrawled 'Gunpowder!' By the flames,
Decked out in crimson, gemmed with syenite,
Hailing their fellows with outrageous names,
The pirates sat and diced. Their eyes were moons.
'Doubloons!' they said. The words crashed gold. 'Doubloons!'

STEPHEN VINCENT BENET

69

The Spring

Now that the winter's gone, the earth hath lost
Her snow-white robes, and now no more the frost
Candies the grass, or casts an icy cream
Upon the silver lake, or crystal stream:
But the warm sun thaws the benumbed earth,
And makes it tender, gives a sacred birth
To the dead swallow; wakes in hollow tree
The drowsy cuckoo, and the bumblebee.
Now does a choir of chirping minstrels bring,
In triumph to the world, the youthful Spring.
The valleys, hills, and woods, in rich array,
Welcome the coming of the longed-for May.

THOMAS CAREW

who knows if the moon's a balloon

who knows if the moon's
a balloon,coming out of a keen city
in the sky—filled with pretty people?
(and if you and i should

get into it,if they
should take me and take you into their balloon,
why then
we'd go up higher with all the pretty people

than houses and steeples and clouds:
go sailing
away and away sailing into a keen
city which nobody's ever visited,where

always
      it's
           Spring)and everyone's
in love and flowers pick themselves

E. E. CUMMINGS

Leli

1   Leli is hoe-ing the soil today—
a little patch beneath the prickly pears;
not for any root crop but, rather, stones;
carefully he sorts, examines and approves, then
casts the favoured stones into a rusted wheelbarrow;
two goats amble up and he—
for a moment a small bronze boy again and not
the fledgling farmer—flails his arms—
chases them and shouts (I am convinced)
in goat language.

Two goats have knocked his barrow over—
again, louder, he shouts
(swearing in Goatish, perhaps)
and fierce anger contains
a fiercer joy.

2   Leli, pilot of the rooftop,
persuades his kite to fly highest of all;
nine kites I counted, reaching to the sun,
with Leli's soaring far above the rest—
far, far higher than the great Rotunda,
his smile of contentment as satisfied
as a honey-brown kitten with a saucer of cream,
vast as the dome itself upturned.

Captain Leli, ace of the go-cart—
tamer of goats and pert Blackie, the puppy—
who conjured up his private wind on
a still and equable day.

NOEL LLOYD

By St Thomas Water

By St Thomas Water
Where the river is thin
We looked for a jam-jar
To catch the quick fish in.
Through St Thomas Church-yard
Jessie and I ran
The day we took the jam-pot
Off the dead man.

On the scuffed tombstone
The grey flowers fell,
Cracked was the water,
Silent the shell.
The snake for an emblem
Swirled on the slab,
Across the beach of sky the sun
Crawled like a crab.

'If we walk,' said Jessie,
'Seven times round,
We shall hear a dead man
Speaking underground.'
Round the stone we danced, we sang,
Watched the sun drop,
Laid our heads and listened
At the tomb-top.

Soft as the thunder
At the storm's start
I heard a voice as clear as blood,
Strong as the heart.
But what words were spoken
I can never say,
I shut my fingers round my head,
Drove them away.

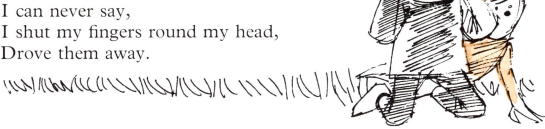

'What are those letters, Jessie,
Cut so sharp and trim
All round this holy stone
With earth up to the brim?'
Jessie traced the letters
Black as coffin-lead.
'*He is not dead but sleeping,*'
Slowly she said.

I looked at Jessie,
Jessie looked at me,
And our eyes in wonder
Grew wide as the sea.
Past the green and bending stones
We fled hand in hand,
Silent through the tongues of grass
To the river strand.

By the creaking cypress
We moved as soft as smoke
For fear all the people
Underneath woke.
Over all the sleepers
We darted light as snow
In case they opened up their eyes,
Called us from below.

Many a day has faltered
Into many a year
Since the dead awoke and spoke
And we would not hear.
Waiting in the cold grass
Under a crinkled bough,
Quiet stone, cautious stone,
What do you tell me now?

CHARLES CAUSLEY

Hide and Seek

Call out. Call loud: 'I'm ready! Come and find me!'
The sacks in the toolshed smell like the seaside.
They'll never find you in this salty dark,
But be careful that your feet aren't sticking out.
Wiser not to risk another shout.
The floor is cold. They'll probably be searching
The bushes near the swing. Whatever happens
You mustn't sneeze when they come prowling in.
And here they are, whispering at the door;
You've never heard them sound so hushed before.
Don't breathe. Don't move. Stay dumb. Hide in your
   blindness.
They're moving closer, someone stumbles, mutters;
Their words and laughter scuffle, and they're gone.
But don't come out just yet; they'll try the lane
And then the greenhouse and back here again.
They must be thinking that you're very clever,
Getting more puzzled as they search all over.
It seems a long time since they went away.
Your legs are stiff, the cold bites through your coat;
The dark damp smell of sand moves in your throat.
It's time to let them know that you're the winner.
Push off the sacks. Uncurl and stretch. That's better!
Out of the shed and call to them: 'I've won!
Here I am! Come and own up I've caught you!'
The darkening garden watches. Nothing stirs.
The bushes hold their breath; the sun is gone.
Yes, here you are. But where are they who sought you?

VERNON SCANNELL

Now the Hungry Lion Roars

Now the hungry lion roars
 And the wolf behowls the moon:
Whilst the heavy ploughman snores,
 All with heavy task fordone.
Now the wasted brands do glow,
 Whilst the screech-owl, screeching loud,
Puts the wretch that lies in woe
 In remembrance of a shroud.
Now it is the time of night,
 That the graves, all gaping wide,
Every one lets forth his sprite,
 In the churchway paths to glide:
And we fairies, that do run
 By the triple Hecate's team,
From the presence of the sun,
 Following darkness like a dream,
Now are frolic: not a mouse
Shall disturb this hallowed house:
I am sent with broom before,
To sweep the dust behind the door.

WILLIAM SHAKESPEARE

78

maggie and milly and molly and may

maggie and milly and molly and may
went down to the beach(to play one day)

and maggie discovered a shell that sang
so sweetly she couldn't remember her troubles,and

milly befriended a stranded star
whose rays five languid fingers were;

and molly was chased by a horrible thing
which raced sideways while blowing bubbles: and

may came home with a smooth round stone
as small as a world and as large as alone.

for whatever we lose(like a you or a me)
it's always ourselves we find in the sea.

E. E. CUMMINGS

FROM **Summer**

The small dust-colour'd beetle climbs with pain
O'er the smooth plantain-leaf, a spacious plain!
Thence higher still, by countless steps convey'd,
He gains the summit of a shiv'ring blade,
And flirts his filmy wings, and looks around,
Exulting in his distance from the ground.
The tender speckled moth here dancing seen,
The vaulting grasshopper of glossy green,
And all prolific *Summer's* sporting train,
Their little lives by various pow'rs sustain.

ROBERT BLOOMFIELD

The Principal Part of a Python

The principal part of a python—
As any one plainly can see—
Is the part that begins in the middle
And goes both ways indefinitely.

The trouble is, no one can tell you
Whether it's tail, sir, or nose.
It simply begins in the middle
And grows and grows and grows.

I think the Python might like it
If someone who knows could decide
When he wriggles along through the jungle
Which end is getting the ride.

Is it tail that is doing the pushing
Wherever the Python goes?
Or does tail just hang there resting
While he wriggles along on his nose?

Don't *you* think the Python might like it
If someone who knows would decide
When he wriggles along through the jungle
Which end is getting the ride?

JOHN CIARDI

81

Who's That?

Who's that
stopping at
my door in the
dark, deep
in the dead of the moonless night?

Who's
that in the quiet
blackness,
darker than dark?

Who
turns the han-
dle of my door, who
turns the old brass hand-
le of
my door with never a sound, the handle
that always
creaks and rattles and
squeaks but
now
turns
without a sound, slowly
slowly
      slowly
           round?

Who's that moving through the floor
as if it were a lake, an open door? Who
is it who passes through
what can never be passed through,
who passes through
the rocking-chair
without rocking it,
who passes through
the table without knocking it, who
walks out of the cupboard without unlocking it?
Who's that? Who plays with my toys
with no noise, no
noise?

Who's that? Who is it
silent and silver
as things in mirrors, who's
as slow as feathers,
shy as the shivers,
light as a fly?

Who's that who's that
as close as
close as a hug, a kiss—

Who's THIS?

JAMES KIRKUP

The Ride-by-Nights

Up on their brooms the Witches stream,
Crooked and black in the crescent's gleam;
One foot high, and one foot low,
Bearded, cloaked, and cowled, they go.

'Neath Charlie's Wain they twitter and tweet,
And away they swarm 'neath the Dragon's feet,
With a whoop and a flutter they swing and sway,
And surge pell-mell down the Milky Way.

Between the legs of the glittering Chair
They hover and squeak in the empty air.
Then round they swoop past the glimmering Lion
To where Sirius barks behind huge Orion;
Up, then, and over to wheel amain
Under the silver, and home again.

WALTER DE LA MARE

Frogs

Frogs sit more solid
Than anything sits. In mid-leap they are
Parachutists falling
In a free fall. They die on roads
With arms across their chests and
Heads high.

I love frogs that sit
Like Buddha, that fall without
Parachutes, that die
Like Italian tenors.

Above all, I love them because,
Pursued in water,
they never
Panic so much that they fail
To make stylish triangles
With their ballet dancer's
Legs.

NORMAN MACCAIG

Me

As long as I live
I shall always be
My Self—and no other.
Just me.

Like a tree—
Willow, elder,
Aspen, thorn,
Or cypress forlorn.

Like a flower,
For its hour—
Primrose, or pink,

Or a violet—
Sunned by the sun,
And with dewdrops wet.

Always just me.
Till the day come on
When I leave this body,
It's all then done.
And the spirit within it
Is gone.

WALTER DE LA MARE

86

Playthings

The evening was green and gold on the water,
Golden and green the palaces
Of the high trees, high on the hill over the stream;
And we were children, whose jewels
Were pebbles under the waves' stir,
In the brown bed where the weeds sway,
Where the fishes gleam.

There was nothing beyond the stream or the children
Or the green swaying, nothing beyond; but within,
Far within, was the secret
That out of delight wove the playing
Of all things, weed, wood and water;
We knelt there, and if we were still
Out of the golden dark, from the secret, came flying
Purest of playthings, the arrow-swift kingfisher flam-
ing,
Swift, swift and blue,
And a fire and a vision
And a world were shut under his wing.

KATHLEEN ABBOTT

On the Grasshopper and Cricket

The poetry of earth is never dead:
  When all the birds are faint with the hot sun,
  And hide in cooling trees, a voice will run
From hedge to hedge about the new-mown mead;
That is the Grasshopper's—he takes the lead
  In Summer luxury; he has never done
  With his delights; for when tired out with fun
He rests at ease beneath some pleasant weed.
The poetry of earth is ceasing never:
On a lone winter evening, when the frost
  Has wrought a silence, from the stove there shrills
The Cricket's song, in warmth increasing ever,
And seems to one in drowsiness half lost,
  The Grasshopper's song among some grassy hills.

JOHN KEATS

88

The Song of Wandering Aengus

I went out to the hazel wood,
Because a fire was in my head,
And cut and peeled a hazel wand,
And hooked a berry to a thread;
And when white moths were on the wing,
And moth-like stars were flickering out,
I dropped the berry in a stream
And caught a little silver trout.

When I had laid it on the floor
I went to blow the fire a-flame,
But something rustled on the floor,
And someone called me by my name:
It had become a glimmering girl
With apple blossom in her hair
Who called me by my name and ran
And faded through the brightening air.

Though I am old with wandering
Through hollow lands and hilly lands,
I will find out where she has gone,
And kiss her lips and take her hands;
And walk among long dappled grass,
And pluck till time and times are done
The silver apples of the moon,
The golden apples of the sun.

W. B. YEATS

Zodiac

What are the Signs of Zodiac,
Marked in stars on Heaven's track?

The Water-Carrier bears on high,
His jar in January's sky.

February brings a pair
Of Fish to swim in dark blue air.

In March a horned Ram doth run
Between the visits of the sun.

April rides upon a Bull
Vigorous and beautiful.

The Twins we call the Gemini
May-month cradles in the sky.

In June the Crab goes crawling o'er
The spaces of the heavenly shore.

Where the Crab no longer creeps,
In July the Lion leaps.

Through August night, like daisy-laden
Meadows, walks a Vestal Maiden.

September, though it blows big gales,
Holds aloft a pair of Scales.

On October's map is shown
A star-bespangled Scorpion.

In November, kneeling low,
See, the Archer bends his bow.

December's frolic is a goat
Bleating in his starry throat.

These are the Signs of Zodiac,
Marking time on Heaven's track.

ELEANOR FARJEON

Something Told the Wild Geese

Something told the wild geese
   It was time to go.
Though the fields lay golden
   Something whispered—'Snow'.
Leaves were green and stirring,
   Berries, lustre-glossed,
But beneath warm feathers
   Something cautioned—'Frost'.

All the sagging orchards
   Steamed with amber spice,
But each wild breast stiffened
   At remembered ice.
Something told the wild geese
   It was time to fly—
Summer sun was on their wings,
   Winter in their cry.

RACHEL FIELD

The Firefly

Mostly I let be, when a snake
is horribly swallowing a frog,
when flocking sparrows peck in anger
out the eyes of a murderous kitten,
I take no sides. The nature of things is deadly.
I shudder, but it does not fascinate me
and I go away, not to put a stop.

Yet I have rescued from the octagonal web
of the pinching spider this sick firefly,
I hope in time. I have taken sides.
For late last night this one or one like him
amazed my lonely room with a blue bolt
of lightning, when I was half asleep.

PAUL GOODMAN

The Christmas Tree

Put out the lights now!
Look at the Tree, the rough tree dazzled
In oriole plumes of flame,
Tinselled with twinkling frost fire, tasselled
With stars and moons—the same
That yesterday hid in the spinney and had no fame
Till we put out the lights now.

Hard are the nights now:
The fields at moonrise turn to agate,
Shadows are cold as jet;
In dyke and furrow, in copse and faggot
The frost's tooth is set;
And stars are the sparks whirled out by the north
   wind's fret
On the flinty nights now.

So feast your eyes now
On mimic star and moon-cold bauble:
Worlds may wither unseen,
But the Christmas Tree is a tree of fable,
A phoenix in evergreen,
And the world cannot change or chill what its
   mysteries mean
To your hearts and eyes now.

The vision dies now
Candle by candle: the tree that embraced it
Returns to its own kind,
To be earthed again and weather as best it
May the frost and wind.
Children, it too had its hour—you will not mind
If it lives or dies now.

C. DAY LEWIS

Joie-de-Vivre

In our house we have a little ray of sunshine.
    It emanates from Carolina Jane.
Though her future may be shady this indomitable lady
    Is never heard to cavil or complain.

There's a streak of bull-dog in Carolina
    That will not let her tolerate a grouse.
When increases in taxation had depressed the British nation,
    She warbled 'Rule Britannia' 'round the house.

She disturbs our morning slumbers with an aria,
    The bathroom is a minor Sadler's Wells;
From the dawning to the dark she's as happy as a lark—
    And expects the same of everybody else.

It's a splendid thing to be optimistic,
    So confident that all's as right as rain;
But her attitude is cloying, and it's apt to be annoying—
    And we're going to murder Carolina Jane!

DOROTHY ROSE GRIBBLE

New Moon

The new moon, of no importance
lingers behind as the yellow sun glares and is gone
    beyond the sea's edge;
earth smokes blue;
the new moon, in cool height above the blushes,
brings a fresh fragrance of heaven to our senses.

D. H. LAWRENCE

A New Year Carol

Here we bring new water from the well so clear,
For to worship God with this happy New Year.
Sing levy dew, the water and the wine;
The seven bright gold wires
And the bugles that do shine.

Sing reign of Fair Maid, with gold upon her toe,
Open you the West Door and turn the Old Year go.
Sing levy dew, the water and the wine;
The seven bright gold wires
And the bugles that do shine.

Sing reign of Fair Maid, with gold upon her chin,
Open you the East Door and let the New Year in.
Sing levy dew, the water and the wine;
The seven bright gold wires
And the bugles that do shine.

UNKNOWN

96

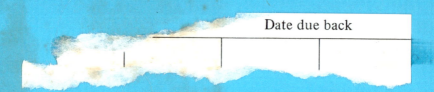

Date due back